THIS CANDLEWICK BOOK BELONGS TO:

_____

_____

_____

For
Mum and Dad, brother Ben,
and Alice
J. F.

Text copyright © 2008 by Jack Foreman   Illustrations copyright © 2008 by Michael Foreman

First U.S. paperback edition 2012

Library of Congress Cataloging-in-Publication Data is available.

Library of Congress Catalog Card Number 2007038143

ISBN 978-0-7636-3657-9 (hardcover)

ISBN 978-0-7636-6087-1 (paperback)

12 13 14 15 16 17 SCP 10 9 8 7 6 5 4 3 2 1

Printed in Humen, Dongguan, China

This book was typeset in Gill Sans.
The illustrations were done in charcoal, colored pencil, and pastel.

Candlewick Press
99 Dover Street
Somerville, Massachusetts 02144

visit us at www.candlewick.com

Say Hello

Jack & Michael Foreman

CANDLEWICK PRESS

Left out.

All alone.

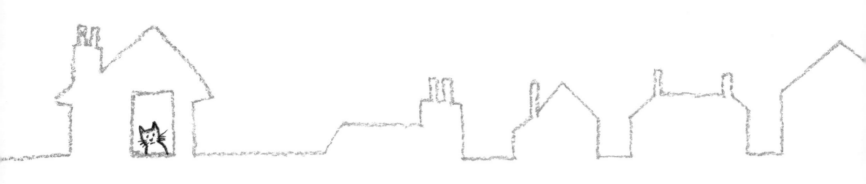

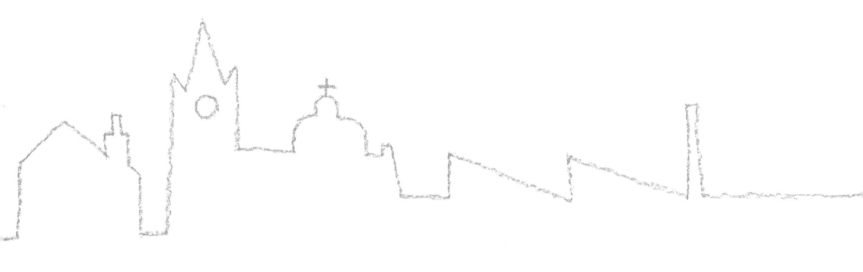

No friend, no home.

What's this?

Can I play too?

It's great to make new friends like you!

Left out, no fun.

Why am I the only one?

Left out, no fun.

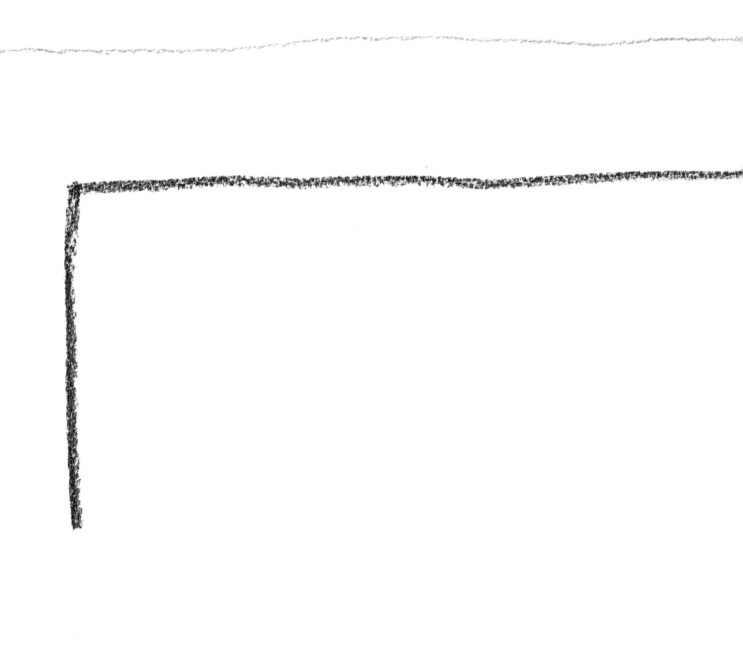

Why am I the lonely one?

Left out, no fun.

I wouldn't do this

to anyone.

What's this?

Come and join the fun!

No need to be the lonely one.

When someone's feeling left out, low,

it doesn't take much to say . . .

ALoha!   ShaLom!   Namaste!

Szia!   Dia duit!   Ciao!

Ave!

Konichiwa!   Olá!   Kia ora!

Sveiki!

cześć!

Hellow!   Labas!   Hei!   Sekoh!

Hola!   Привет!   你好

Jambo!   Salaam!   Helō!